*To Michael, Dave and Truffles*

Copyright text © 1997 Cheryl Uhrig.
Copyright illustration © 1997 Cheryl Uhrig

Written and illustrated by Cheryl E. Uhrig

Printed in Canada by Kempenfelt Graphics
(Barrie, Ontario)

No part of this publication may be reproduced on whole or in part, stored in a retrieval system or transmitted in any form or by any means without written permission from the publisher.

ISBN 0-9681925-3-x

• ALL RIGHTS RESERVED •

2

Truffles was a wonderful dog. She was white, blonde, brown and black, with two floppy ears, a long furry face and a tail that looked like an old feather duster.

BIRTH TO FIVE

Truffles lived in a cosy little house with a Mom and a Dad who loved her very much. Each night before she went to bed, Truffles thought she was the luckiest dog in the whole wide world.

Then one night the Mom sat up in bed and said, "Oh my! I think it's time." At which point the Dad sat up. Then he jumped up and ran around the room as fast as he could yelling,

**"IT'S TIME! IT'S TIME!"**

Well after the Dad calmed down, the Mom grabbed a little bag from the closet. Then they both got in the car and drove off.

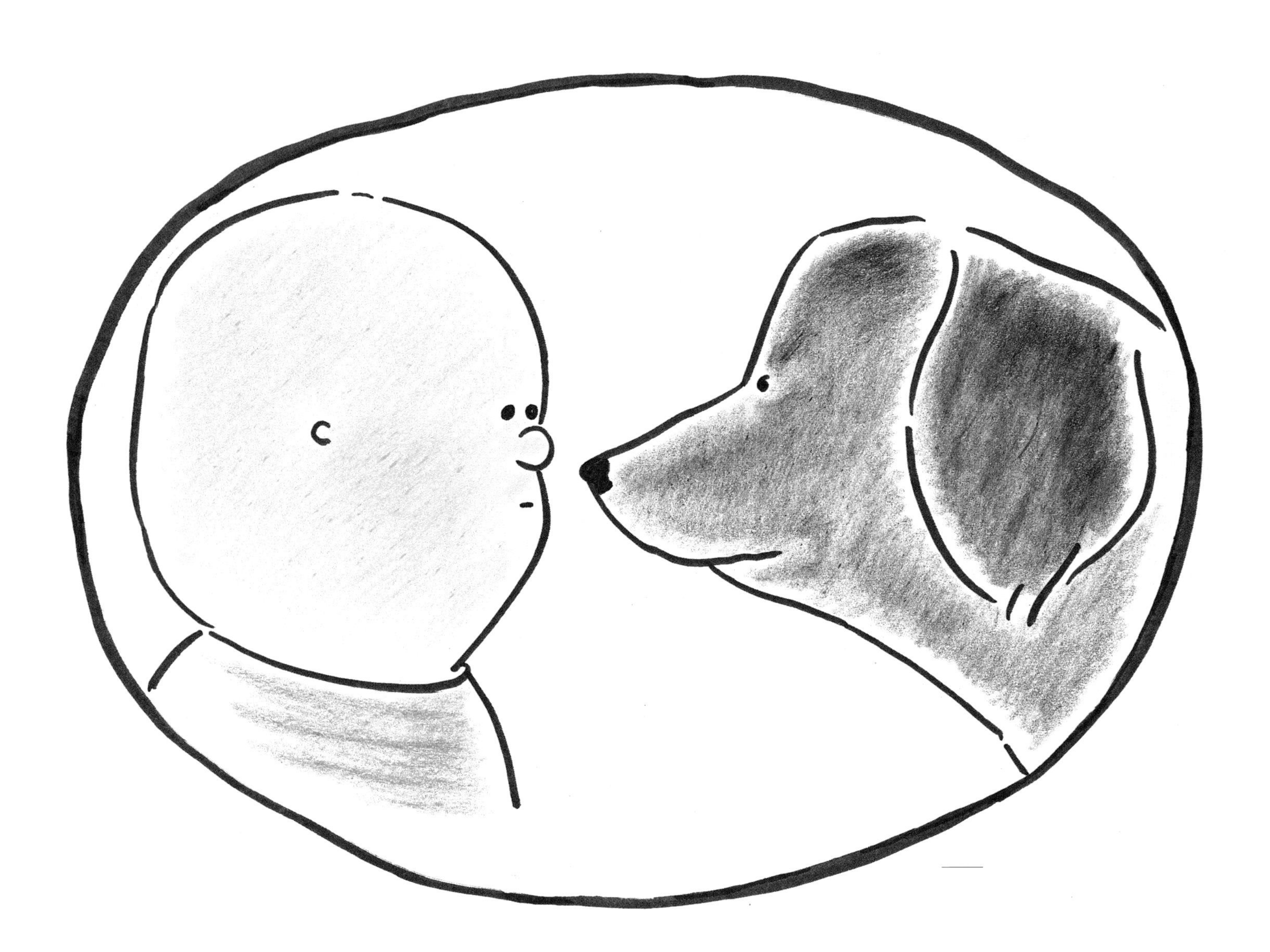

Now just when Truffles thought the Mom and the Dad were never coming home again...they came home. But with them came a baby.
**A little baby boy.**

**"Oohh. aahh,"** said all the neighbours, the grandparents, the aunts and uncles and their friends. **"Oohh, Nnoo!"** thought Truffles as she pushed her way through the crowd.

Well that little baby boy slept and cried, cried and laughed. But aside from the odd sleepless night, Truffles still thought she was the luckiest dog in the whole wide world.

M E O

However, it wasn't long before that baby started to grow and move, move and touch. Until one day he reached over to Truffles, and gave her head a **bop.** Then **another bop.** Luckily, just before he gave her the **biggest bop of all,** the Mom rushed over and said,**"Please don't bug the dog."** Then she turned to Truffles and said, "Don't worry Truffles, some day he will be your very best friend."

Well that little baby boy grew and crawled, crawled and stood up. Until one day he stood up, grabbed Truffles right on the end of her nose and gave it a **twist,** and then **another twist.** Luckily, just before he gave it the **biggest twist of all,** the Mom rushed over and said,**"Please don't bug the dog."** Then she turned to Truffles and said, "Don't worry Truffles, some day he will be your very best friend."

Well that little boy grew and walked, walked and talked. Until one day he jumped on Truffles' back, yelled, "Giddyup Horsey" and gave her a **kick.** Then **another kick.** Luckily, just before he gave her the **biggest kick of all,** the Mom rushed over and said,**"Please don't bug the dog."** Then she turned to Truffles and said, "Don't worry Truffles, some day he will be your very best friend."

Well that little boy grew and ran, ran and played. Until one day he played with Truffles. He opened her mouth and said, **“Say ahh.”** Then he said, **“Say aahh” again.** Luckily, just before he made her say the **biggest ‘aaahhh’ of all,** the Mom rushed over and said,**“Please don’t bug the dog.”** Then she turned to Truffles and said,“Don’t worry Truffles, some day he will be your very best friend.”

'TRUFF'

Well that little boy grew and turned four. Then he grew some more. Until one day he went to the cupboard where Truffles' food was kept. He poured her breakfast, filled her bowl with fresh water, and said, "Mom, could we please take Truffles for a walk?" Now the Mom bent over, hugged her very grown-up little boy as long as she could without bugging him and said,"Of course we can."

Then she turned to Truffles and said,

**"See Truffles, we told you he would be your very best friend."**

Once again Truffles was a happy dog. She had a Mom, a Dad, and a wonderful little boy who loved her very much. Each night before Truffles went to bed, she thought she was the luckiest dog in the whole wide world. Until one night she heard the Mom in the next room say, **"Oh my. I think it's time!"** Then the Dad jumped up and ran around the room as fast as he could yelling, **"IT'S TIME! IT'S TIME!"** But before Truffles could make a run for it, the little boy ran over to Truffles, gave her a great big hug and said, **"Don't worry Truffles, some day that baby will be your very best friend."**

**And one day...she was.**

The end.